HILARY AND THE RICH GIRL

HILARY AND THE RICH GIRL

Suzanne Weyn

SCHOLASTIC INC.
New York Toronto London Auckland Sydney

ISBN 0-590-43560-4

12 11 10 9 8 7 6 5 4 3 2 1 1 2 3 4 5 6/9

Printed in the U.S.A. 28

First Scholastic printing, August 1991

1

The Most Beautiful Girl in Wild Falls

HILARY BAKER WAITED at the school bus stop. Beside her were ten of her eleven brothers and sisters. The Baker kids were the only ones who waited at that stop.

The bus stop was on a country road, just a short walk away from the Bakers' big gray house.

"I hate waiting for the bus," said Hilary. "My legs are tired. They should put some benches here."

"Complain, complain, complain," said Collette Baker. "That's all you ever do." Collette picked a piece of leaf from her thick black braid. "Sometimes you drive me crazy," she added.

Like Hilary, Collette was eight. So were Patty, Olivia, and Kenny Baker. All the Baker kids were adopted, and some of them were the same age.

A boy ran behind Hilary. "You can't catch me, ninja master!" cried Howie Baker. He pushed his glasses back up on his nose.

"Oh, yes I can!" said Kevin Baker.

Howie was seven and Kevin was six. Today they were pretending to be characters from a comic book.

Kevin leaped in front of Hilary. His mop of red curls bounced as he chased Howie. "I am the ninja master of power!"

"Would you guys get out of here!" cried Hilary.

"I have to go to the bathroom," said

five-year-old Jack. He was in kindergarten.

"Hold on, Jack," said Terry. She was also seven. "The bus will be here soon. Ask Mrs. Therm as soon as you get to school, okay?"

"Here comes the bus," said pretty Christine Baker. Christine was a teenager, and the oldest Baker kid.

The bus pulled up to the stop. Everyone got on but Christine and Mark. Mark was twelve. He and Christine took another bus to the Wild Falls Junior High and High Schools.

Today, Hilary had a problem. She usually sat with her friend Marissa. But Marissa had gone into the hospital to have her tonsils removed.

"Want to sit with me today?" Hilary asked her newest sister, Patty. The Bakers had adopted her only a month and a half ago.

"Okay," Patty agreed. "It's better than sitting with Snoddy Goldleaf."

Snoddy was a fifth-grader, the worst fifth-grader in Wild Falls Elementary. Since Patty was new, she always got stuck sitting with him.

"Yesterday Snoddy had ants in his pencil case," Patty told Hilary. "He put one in my hair."

Hilary giggled.

"Oh, yuck! Don't laugh," said Patty, glancing back at the stocky boy. "It was disgusting."

The bus traveled along curvy country roads. It made its final stop in the downtown part of town.

This morning, a new girl got on.

She had long blonde hair and bright blue eyes, and wore a furry white coat.

Hilary stared at her. *She's the most beautiful girl in Wild Falls,* she thought.

"Poor girl. She has to sit with Snoddy," Patty whispered to Hilary. "It's the only seat left."

The new girl took her seat next to

Snoddy Goldleaf. She didn't even look at him.

Finally, the bus pulled into the school parking lot. Patty got up to leave. But Hilary didn't. She wanted to meet the new girl.

"Aren't you coming?" Patty asked Hilary.

"Uh, no," said Hilary. "You go ahead." She planned to let the new girl pass by her seat. Then she would walk out behind her.

"Are you staying on the bus all day?" Patty asked.

"I'll be there in a minute," said Hilary.

"You're weird," shrugged Patty as she walked up the aisle.

Hilary waited until the new girl stood by her side. Then she got up and stepped into the aisle.

"Hey, watch it!" cried Snoddy Goldleaf. "You stomped on my foot, beak nose!"

Beak nose! Hilary had never liked her nose. She thought it was a little too pointy. Still, she told herself that no one else noticed it.

Leave it to Snoddy Goldleaf to notice.

"Hey, Snodgrass, leave her alone," came a voice from the back of the bus. It was Kenny Baker. He had called Snoddy by his full name, Snodgrass. That was a sure way to get him mad.

Snoddy's face turned red. "You gonna make me?" he cried.

"If I have to," Kenny answered.

"Hey, no fighting back there," called Mr. Fisher, the bus driver. "Keep moving."

Hilary saw that the new girl was no longer ahead of her. She'd gotten off the bus already. Quickly, Hilary hurried to catch up.

Hilary looked around the schoolyard until she spotted the new girl at the other end of the yard. She was talking to Hilary's third-grade teacher, Ms. Sherman.

The school bell rang, and the kids all lined up in pairs. Patty, Collette, and Olivia were also in Ms. Sherman's third-grade class. Mr. Popol was Kenny's third-grade teacher. Hilary joined Patty, Collette, and Olivia at the end of the line.

When they got inside, Hilary saw the new girl standing at the front of the class with Ms. Sherman.

"Class, this is Alice Birmingham," Ms. Sherman announced. "Her family just moved to Wild Falls. Will someone be in charge of showing Alice around today?"

Hilary's arm shot up in the air.

"Hilary Baker," said Ms. Sherman.

Hilary smiled her best smile at Alice Birmingham.

Alice's lips twitched. It wasn't much of a smile. *She's just scared because she's new,* thought Hilary. *I'll help her get over that.*

Alice went to her seat. The class took out their social studies books. Hilary peeked at the girl from the corner of her eye. Alice peeked back. She saw Hilary looking at her. She quickly looked down at her book.

I bet she's shy, thought Hilary. *After a few minutes with me she'll feel right at home.*

2

The Cool Table

THE LUNCH BELL rang. Hilary hopped out of her seat. "We'll be partners on the lunch line," she told Alice.

"All right," said Alice.

The two girls took their coats from the coat closet and got in line. Ms. Sherman led the class downstairs to the lunchroom.

Most days Hilary sat at a table with Olivia, Collette, and Patty. Some other friends usually joined them. But today Hilary wanted Alice all to herself.

"Come on," she said. "Let's sit over there at that empty table."

Alice gazed around the room. "Can't we sit with some other kids?" she asked. "What about those girls?"

Hilary gulped. Alice had pointed toward Kimberly Berry and Jessica Harmon, two of the richest, prettiest girls in her class. And two of the snobbiest!

"Okay," said Hilary, taking a deep breath. She hoped Jessica and Kimberly wouldn't tell her to get lost.

"Hi," she greeted the two girls. "Mind if we sit with you?"

"I don't mind," said Jessica.

"Me neither," added Kimberly.

Alice and Hilary sat down at their table. Hilary was proud to sit with these girls. She hoped everyone in the lunchroom noticed.

Suddenly, Alice didn't seem shy anymore. She had lots to say to Kimberly and Jessica. They talked about the Wild

Falls Country Club, a fancy club that all their families belonged to. It sounded like a wonderful place. But the Bakers didn't belong. Hilary had nothing to say.

"Let's go outside," said Jessica when they'd finished their lunch. "I'll show you our part of the schoolyard. We like to hang out near the far end."

"Ms. Sherman told *me* to show her around," Hilary objected.

"That's okay," said Alice. "You don't have to anymore. Jessica and Kimberly can show me where everything is."

"But . . . but . . ." Hilary said. The three girls ignored her. They got up and put on their coats.

"We want to show Alice around while we still have time," said Jessica. "See ya later."

"Okay, see ya," Hilary replied. They took their trays and left Hilary sitting all alone.

* * *

After school, Hilary went straight home. As soon as she got in the door, she called to her mother, "Mom!"

"In the kitchen," her mother called back.

Hilary went to the kitchen. Mrs. Baker was unloading the dishwasher. Her thick golden hair was tied back in a fat braid. She wore jeans and a big gray sweat-shirt.

"Mom, why don't we belong to the Wild Falls Country Club?" Hilary asked.

"Because that's a club for rich people," her mother answered "It costs a lot of money to join."

"Does that mean we're poor?" asked Hilary.

Mrs. Baker thought for a moment. "No, we are definitely not poor," she said. "When we first adopted you, we didn't have a lot. But then Dad inherited some money. So we were able to adopt your brothers and sisters."

"But we're not rich," said Hilary.

"No, I'm afraid we're somewhere in the middle."

"But my other mom and dad were rich. What happened to all their money?" asked Hilary.

Hilary's natural parents had died in a sailing accident. Tom and Ann Baker had been their friends. They adopted Hilary after the accident.

"We'll use some of that money to pay for your college. The rest will be yours when you're twenty-one," said Mrs. Baker.

"Can I get some of the money now?" asked Hilary.

"Why? What do you need money for?" asked Mrs. Baker.

"Nothing special," Hilary told her. "I just want to be rich now. That's all."

Just then, Terry burst into the kitchen. "Mom! Mom! Mom!" she cried. "Look at this!" She held a newspaper in her hands.

Small, blonde Terry was the quietest of the Bakers. Sometimes the others forgot she was even there. So when Terry made noise, everyone listened.

Patty, Olivia, Collette, Kenny, and Mark hurried into the kitchen. "What's the matter?" asked Olivia.

"Nothing's the matter," said Terry. As she spoke, her tongue peeked through her two missing front teeth. "The ice show is coming to town!"

Patty took the paper from Terry. " 'The American Ice Show. At the Upstate Sports Arena,' " she read.

Mark came to Patty's side. He looked at the paper. "Tony Jones is skating!" he cried. "He played hockey for the Redbirds."

"Let's see," said Mrs. Baker. Patty handed her the paper. Mrs. Baker sat down at the table and spread out the full-page ad. All the kids crowded around, looking over her shoulder.

Howie and Kevin ran into the kitchen

to see what was going on. “Superhero skaters!” yelled Howie. He pointed to a picture in the ad of comic book heroes battling on the ice.

“Debbie Grace is skating,” said Collette, reading the paper. “She won a silver medal in the Olympics. Remember?”

“It was like ballet when she skated,” Hilary recalled. Hilary hoped to be a ballerina someday.

Christine came into the kitchen with three-year-old Dixie. Dixie climbed onto Mrs. Baker’s lap. “Berry Bears!” Dixie cried.

The Berry Bears were Dixie’s favorite cartoon characters. In the picture, people dressed as the Berry Bears were skating.

“Can we go, Mom?” asked Terry.

“I think so. Sure,” said Mrs. Baker. She looked down at the bottom of the page. “Fifteen dollars a ticket!” she cried.

Howie pushed his glasses back up on his nose. "I'll figure it out," he said. Howie was a whiz in math and science. "There are fourteen of us. Do you think Grannie Baker will want to go?"

"No, she doesn't get back from her vacation in China until next month," Mrs. Baker told him.

"Then I won't count her," said Howie. "Fourteen times fifteen is . . . is . . . two hundred and ten."

"I don't care if I go," offered Christine.

Mrs. Baker smiled at her. "I don't have to go, either," she said. "Your father can take you. Anyone else *not* want to go?"

No one said anything.

"If you two don't go, then it will cost one hundred and eighty dollars," Howie figured.

Mrs. Baker shook her head sadly. "I'm sorry, kids. I don't think we can afford it."

Darn! thought Hilary. *If I were rich right now, I could take everyone.*

"I really wanted to see Tony Jones, too," grumbled Mark.

Christine gazed at the ad. "I have an idea," she said. "The show isn't until next week. What if we all put in our allowances and extra money? Maybe we can pay for the tickets ourselves."

"I have some birthday money," said Olivia.

"And I got two dollars when I lost my teeth," added Terry.

Mrs. Baker got up. She took a cookie tin from a high shelf. "I've saved seventy dollars in here," she said, opening the tin. "I'll donate it to the ice show fund. You kids will have to come up with the rest."

"We can do it," said Collette.

"Patty, will you be in charge of collecting the money?" said Mrs. Baker.

"All right," Patty agreed, pleased to have the job.

Mrs. Baker handed her the tin. "Here. You can put the money in this," she said. "I'll keep the seventy until you're ready."

A tall man with wispy blond hair came through the back door. "Hi, kids," said Mr. Baker. He leaned over and gave Mrs. Baker a kiss.

"Hey, Dad," said Kevin. "We're all going to the ice show."

Mr. Baker didn't smile. "How much is that going to cost us?" he asked his wife.

"Not much, dear," said Mrs. Baker. "We've got it all under control."

"Good," said Mr. Baker. "Now I want to see some homework action."

The kids ran out of the kitchen. Hilary caught up with Patty. "I bet Alice Birmingham doesn't have to pay for her own ice show ticket," said Hilary as they climbed the stairs.

"So? What if she doesn't?" said Patty. "Who cares?"

I care, thought Hilary. It wasn't fair

that she lived in a home where the kids had to pay for their own treats. It was all a terrible mistake. She didn't belong in this house. She belonged at the Wild Falls Country Club with Alice Birmingham.

3

Rich Hilary

THE NEXT MORNING Patty sat down beside Hilary on the bus. "Can't you sit somewhere else?" said Hilary.

Patty screwed up her freckled face and crossed her green eyes. Then she stuck her tongue out at Hilary.

"I'm serious," said Hilary.

Patty folded her arms. "It's a free country," she said. "I can sit where I want. And I'm *not* sitting next to Snoddy." The only other empty seat was the one next to Snoddy.

Hilary sighed. She didn't want to sit with Patty. She wanted Alice to sit next to her instead.

The bus drove on toward town.

Hilary noticed an orange thermos laying on top of Patty's knapsack. "What's that for?" she asked Patty.

"Juice," said Patty. "If I bring my own juice, I can save thirty-five cents a day. I'll give the money I save to the ice show collection."

The bus pulled up to the town stop. Alice got on.

Hilary glanced at Patty from the corner of her eye. She had an idea. A not-very-nice idea.

Hilary picked up Patty's thermos. "I never saw this thermos before," she said.

"It was in the kitchen cabinet," Patty answered. "I found it when — "

"Ooops!" said Hilary as she dropped the thermos. "Sorry." The thermos rolled to the back of the bus.

"Klutz!" said Patty. "I bet you broke

it!" She got up and chased her thermos down the aisle.

Hilary picked up the knapsack. She held it on her own lap.

Alice Birmingham was about to sit down next to Snoddy. "Come sit here, Alice," Hilary called to her.

"All right," said Alice. She sat down beside Hilary.

"Hilary!" cried Patty when she saw Alice in her seat. "I was sitting — "

"Get in your seat!" called Mr. Fisher.

"You got up," said Hilary, trying to sound sweet.

"I'm not moving until everyone is seated," said Mr. Fisher.

Glaring at Hilary, Patty sat down next to Snoddy.

"Don't worry. I have your stuff," Hilary said.

Patty glared at her even harder.

Hilary turned and tried to ignore Patty. "How do you like Wild Falls so far?" Hilary asked Alice.

"Okay, I guess," said Alice. "Jessica told me that girl there is your sister. She said you have two other sisters in class, too. How come you don't eat lunch with them?"

"They're all adopted," Hilary said. "We don't really have much in common."

"Jessica says you're adopted," said Alice.

Big mouth Jessica, Hilary thought angrily. "Yes, but I never lived in a shelter or an orphanage or anything," Hilary said. "My parents were killed while sailing. They were real rich."

"That's nice," said Alice. "I mean, it's too bad that they're dead. But it's nice that they were rich."

Alice looked down at her books. She folded her thin fingers and then unfolded them. "Does that mean you're rich?" she asked.

Hilary saw new interest in Alice's eyes. Suddenly Hilary knew how to make

Alice like her. "Yes," Hilary said. "I inherited everything."

"Really?" said Alice. "You don't look rich."

"Ummm . . . I don't want to make the others feel bad," said Hilary.

Alice nodded. "Girls who have less stuff always want you to share with them," she said. "But it's not fair. Not when your things are so much nicer than theirs."

"That is exactly the problem," said Hilary. "Not many people understand it. I'm so glad you do."

I'm a genius! thought Hilary proudly. She had found just the thing to make Alice like her. Alice was acting much nicer than she had yesterday.

And it's almost true, thought Hilary. In thirteen more years she would have a lot of money. Didn't that make her a rich person — even though she didn't actually have the money yet?

"I'm glad I'm getting to know you

better," said Alice. "What are you doing after school today?"

Hilary's heart thumped excitedly. "Nothing," she said.

"Would you like to come to my nouse? My mother is picking me up after school."

Hilary didn't want to seem too excited. "I suppose so," she said calmly. But inside, she was jumping for joy.

It had started badly — but now it was happening. This was the beginning of their wonderful friendship.

At lunchtime Hilary ate with Alice, Jessica, and Kimberly. The three girls talked about a new fashion doll named Tessie. All of them owned one. Hilary didn't.

Hilary bit into her apple. She listened as the girls chatted about the doll. She didn't mind being left out of the talk now. After school, she would have Alice all to herself.

The rest of the afternoon went slowly for Hilary. When the bell rang, she gathered her books quickly and ran back to the coat closet.

Olivia was putting on her jacket. "Tell Mom I won't be home until supper-time," said Hilary. "I'm going to Alice's house."

"You're supposed to ask Mom first," said Olivia.

"Just tell her, okay?" said Hilary. She didn't want to take the chance of calling home. What if her mother said she couldn't go? No, this way was better.

Collette joined them. "You were so mean to Patty this morning," she said. "Snoddy put two worms in her coat pocket."

"It's none of your business," snapped Hilary. She grabbed her jacket and met up with Alice.

They went out to the schoolyard with the other kids. "There's Mom," said Alice. A blonde woman hurried across the schoolyard toward them. She had on a fur jacket and jeans.

Mrs. Birmingham talked with Ms. Sherman. Then she came and got Alice and Hilary. "Where are your other friends?" she asked.

Other friends?

Then Hilary saw Jessica and Kimberly coming toward them. Her heart sank, but she forced herself to keep smiling.

They all got into Mrs. Birmingham's shiny car. In a few minutes they pulled up a long drive. Alice's house was very big.

They walked up the front steps and went inside. Thick white carpeting covered the floors, and all the furniture looked brand-new. Alice led the girls upstairs to her room.

"What a beautiful bedroom!" cried Hilary.

In the center of the room stood a canopy bed. The pink-checked canopy matched the pink-checked bedspread.

Hilary felt an ache of longing in her chest. This was the room of her dreams. Why couldn't she have a room like this?

Alice opened her tall closet. "These dresses!" Hilary cried. "They're so gorgeous!" Velvet dresses, lace dresses. They hung neatly side by side. One lovelier than the next.

Hilary touched a soft pink velvet dress. Then she remembered that Kimberly, Jessica, and Alice were watching.

"I have dresses just like this," Hilary said.

"I've never seen them," said Kimberly.

"I don't wear them to school," Hilary replied. "Do you think I want to ruin them?"

Alice took a pink case from the bottom of her closet. "You have the Tessie wardrobe!" cried Jessica. "Oh, you're so lucky."

Alice knelt on her pink rug and opened the fat case. It was full of doll clothes all hanging neatly on a rod.

Hilary thought of the fashion dolls at her house. Somehow their hair always got mussed, and their clothes were usually all over the place.

Even the dolls at Alice's house had a better life than at the Baker house!

"What I really want is the Tessie Dreamhouse," said Alice. "I hope I get it for my birthday. If someone gave me that, I would be her best friend forever."

"When is your birthday, exactly?" asked Hilary.

"This Saturday," Alice said. "I'm having a huge party. It's terrible to move to a new place when it's almost your birthday. You don't know who to invite. Of course, all of you are invited. You have to tell me who else I should ask."

The girls spent the next hour making up a guest list. They told Alice which girls would probably bring nice gifts and which ones wouldn't.

"What about your sisters?" Alice

asked. "You don't want them to come, do you?"

"Definitely not," Hilary answered. She was surprised at how guilty she felt when she said that. But she couldn't tell Alice to invite them. She wanted Alice to think of her as separate from the rest of her family. And richer.

Finally, Hilary looked up at the clock on Alice's dresser. "My gosh! It's five o'clock already," Hilary cried. "I have to go."

"How are you going to get home?" asked Alice.

"Gee," said Hilary. "I thought your mother would drive me."

4

Trouble and More Trouble

HILARY SAT IN THE VAN beside her father. Mrs. Birmingham hadn't offered to drive her home. So she had to call her father to come get her.

Were Jessica, Kimberly, and Alice making fun of the van right now? Were they giggling over how old and dented it was? Hilary didn't want to think about it.

At the moment, she had another problem to deal with. She was in trouble.

"Hilary, why didn't you call to let us know where you were?" Mr. Baker asked when they stopped for a light.

"I told Olivia," Hilary said. "Didn't she tell you?"

"She told us," replied Mr. Baker. "But she didn't know where Alice lived. Or her phone number."

"I forgot to tell her," Hilary lied.

"That's no excuse," said Mr. Baker.

They pulled into the driveway and walked in the front door. The sounds of clanking dishes and many voices talking at once came from the kitchen. The family was eating supper.

"Am I punished?" Hilary asked.

Mr. Baker nodded.

"You want me to go to my room now?"

"Yes," he answered. "I'll send someone up with your supper."

Hilary headed up the stairs.

On the third floor, Hilary pushed

open her bedroom door. As usual, Patty's side of the room was neat. *That's because she's lived in so many places,* thought Hilary, kicking off her shoes.

Before coming to the Bakers' house, Patty had lived in two foster homes and a children's shelter. *I suppose you have to be neat when you're always living in someone else's house,* Hilary decided.

Hilary felt proud of her messy half of the room. It proved that she really belonged here. There was no reason to be on company behavior. She was home.

It had taken Hilary about a year to feel this way. She'd been four when her parents died. The first year had been hard. She kept expecting her parents to come back and get her. They had planned to be away for just the weekend.

Two days had turned into forever.

Hilary went to her dresser and yanked at the top drawer. It was so crammed with clothing that it didn't budge. She jiggled the drawer and pulled. That usually worked.

This is Patty's fault, thought Hilary as she jiggled. Before Patty arrived, Hilary had had two dressers. Now she had to jam her things into one, while Patty used the other.

At the bottom of the drawer, Hilary found what she was searching for: a plain gold frame with a picture of a man and woman standing on a dock.

The smiling man and woman were Hilary's first parents.

Flopping down on her bed, Hilary gazed at the photograph. Then she shut her eyes. The picture stayed in her mind. Only this picture was slightly different. In this picture, Hilary stood between her parents.

If they were still alive, she would be rich.

But they weren't. So Hilary was poor. Or in the middle.

It was so unfair. No one knew how hard it was to be a rich person stuck in a poor person's life.

At lunchtime the next day, Hilary once again sat with Alice, Kimberly, and Jessica. They were busy talking about the indoor pool at the Wild Falls Country Club.

Hilary gazed around the room. She saw Kenny coming toward her. He stopped at her table. "Hilary, has puke-face Snoddy bothered you today?" he asked.

"No. What's going on?"

"Oh, I've just been hearing things," Kenny said, looking over his shoulder. "Snoddy's been saying today's the day he declares war on the Bakers."

"He'd better not," said Hilary. "Just let him try to — " Suddenly Hilary stopped. A chocolate cupcake was hurtling through the air toward them. "Kenny, look out!" cried Hilary.

Thwap!

The cupcake hit Kenny on the side of the face.

"Ah-hah! Hah-hah!" Snoddy Goldleaf shrieked with laughter.

Kenny grabbed Hilary's peanut-butter-and-jelly sandwich and threw it. The jelly half fell to the floor. But the peanut-butter half stuck to Snoddy's shirt.

Snoddy's face turned red with anger. He grabbed an open carton of milk and hurled it.

Hilary's eyes went wide with horror. Kenny had stepped aside. Alice was being sprayed with milk.

"My dress!" Alice shrieked and jumped to her feet.

Olivia, Patty, and Collette came running to the table. "You'd better stop it, Snoddy!" Collette cried.

"Yeah. Get out of here, Snoddy!" yelled Hilary. She picked up Jessica's yogurt and threw it at Snoddy.

It flew past Snoddy's shoulder. The yogurt hit a boy on the table across the way.

"Food fight!" yelled the boy.

The next thing Hilary knew, food was flying everywhere. Potato chips, sandwiches, desserts.

Collette threw a fruit pie at Snoddy. Collette herself was smeared with jelly.

Suddenly there was a shrill whistle.

Tweeeeeeeeeeeeeeeeeeeeeeeeeettttttttttttt!!!!!

All the food stopped flying.

It was Mrs. Arnold, the head lunch monitor. She always carried a silver whistle. And that whistle always meant someone was in trouble.

"What is the meaning of this?" she boomed.

No one said a word.

"All right," said Mrs. Arnold. "Let's take a little trip down to the principal's office."

Alice's hand flew to her mouth. "The principal," she gasped.

"Yes, sweetie, the principal," said Mrs. Arnold.

Mrs. Arnold lined up Snoddy, Kenny, Collette, Patty, Olivia, Jessica, Kimberly, Alice, and Hilary along with five other kids.

Everyone watched as the group walked through the lunchroom.

Alice was in front of Hilary on line. Hilary noticed that her slender shoulders were shaking. She was making small whimpery sounds.

"I'm sorry, Alice," Hilary whispered. "This is all my fault."

"It sure is," Alice replied harshly. "I never want to speak to you again."

5

Broken Bones and Crime

WHY IT IS WRONG to waste food, by Hilary Baker. That was as far as Hilary had gotten in her punishment assignment.

Patty had the same punishment. She sat across the room on her bed. Her hand never stopped moving as she wrote.

She seemed to have a lot to say on the subject. Hilary was dying to ask Patty what she was writing.

But she couldn't. Patty was mad at her.

And Hilary was mad at Patty.

In fact, she was mad at everyone who had been in the food fight. They had embarrassed her in front of Alice.

Now Alice wasn't even speaking to her.

Patty sensed that Hilary was looking at her. She looked up, and their eyes met. Patty stuck out her tongue. Hilary did the same. Then Patty went back to her writing.

Hilary stared at the blank page in front of her. *If you waste food, then you will have to go out and buy more,* she wrote. What else was there to say? Hilary couldn't think of anything. It would have to do.

Downstairs, the front door opened and closed. Hilary jumped off her bed. She bolted down the stairs.

Mrs. Baker stood in the hall. She had a shopping bag in one hand and a grocery bag in the other.

Hilary stopped in the middle of the steps. "Did you get it?" she asked excitedly.

"Yes, I got you a present for Alice's party," said Mrs. Baker. Mr. Baker came into the hall and took the groceries from her.

"Did you remember to get red peppers?" he asked, as they headed into the kitchen.

"Yes, I remembered the peppers," she said.

Who cares about peppers? thought Hilary. She ran after her parents into the kitchen. "Let me see the present," she said.

Mrs. Baker reached into the shopping bag. She pulled out a long, flat box. Under the clear wrapper was a doll's party dress, shoes, and a handbag. She gave it to Hilary.

Hilary's face fell. "You were supposed to get the Tessie Dreamhouse," she said.

How could her mother have made this mistake? Hilary had told her — at least ten times — exactly what to buy.

"Sorry, sweetheart," her mother answered. "The Dreamhouse cost over forty dollars."

"So?" said Hilary.

"So, that's too much money to spend on one birthday present. I don't even buy forty-dollar presents for my own family."

"You don't?" Hilary said, surprised.

Mrs. Baker began putting away groceries. Mr. Baker was slicing a red pepper. He was making chili for supper. "Now you've revealed our terrible secret, Ann," he teased Mrs. Baker. "We give cheap gifts."

Mrs. Baker rolled her eyes. "Sad, but true," she said.

"It's not funny!" yelled Hilary. "I can't give Alice this! It's not even a real Tessie dress. It says, 'fits most fashion dolls.' "

"Hilary, I'm sure Alice doesn't expect — " began Mrs. Baker.

"She doesn't expect a crummy gift!" cried Hilary. "Everyone will laugh if I bring a stupid thing like this."

"Hilary," Mr. Baker warned sternly. "Watch that tone of voice."

At that moment, Terry came into the room. She looked at the doll outfit in Hilary's hand. "What a pretty dress," she said.

"Here, it's yours!" said Hilary. She shoved the box into Terry's hands. Blinded with tears, Hilary ran from the kitchen.

Now she would never win back Alice's friendship! She couldn't even show her face at the party. Not with *that* present.

Hilary ran to her bedroom. Patty looked up from the book she was reading.

"What's wrong?" she asked, forgetting their fight for the moment.

"Mom won't buy the Tessie Dreamhouse for Alice's birthday!" Hilary blurted.

"You're crying over *that!*" said Patty. "What is the big deal about Alice? I think she's stuck-up."

"She's not. Alice is high-class. You wouldn't know a high-class person if you fell over one," Hilary replied.

"Be quiet, Hilary. You're bugging me," said Patty. She got off her bed and knelt beside it. She took out the cookie tin Mrs. Baker had given her for collecting ice show money. "I'm going to make my collection now. Do you have any money?" Patty asked.

"I'm afraid not," Hilary sniffed.

Patty counted the money in the tin. "Forty-five dollars."

Just then, there was a loud thud in the hall, followed by a piercing scream.

Hilary and Patty rushed into the hall. Kevin lay sprawed on the floor holding his arm. Tears flowed down his cheeks.

Howie hopped around anxiously beside him. "We were playing ninja. He was trying to do a somersault off the wall."

Patty put down the money tin and ran to Kevin. "Do you think it's broken?" she asked, tenderly touching his arm.

"Aaaaahhhhh!" shrieked Kevin, crying harder. "Don't touch it. It hurts!"

In the next second, Mr. and Mrs. Baker raced up the third-floor steps. "What happened?" cried Mrs. Baker.

"He fell on his arm," Patty told them.

Everyone had heard the scream. Soon all the Baker children were crowded around Kevin.

"I think it's broken," said Mr. Baker after he looked at Kevin's arm.

"Will they cut it off?" asked Jack.

"No! Not my arm!" yelled Kevin.

"No one is cutting Kevin's arm off," said Mr. Baker. Gently, he helped Kevin to his feet.

"Oh, cool! You get to wear a cast now," said Kenny.

"I don't care! Make it stop hurting," sobbed Kevin.

"Let's get you to the hospital," Mr. Baker said, putting his arm around Kevin.

Everyone went downstairs with Kevin and Mr. Baker.

Hilary was about to follow. Then something sitting on the floor caught her eye. It was the cookie tin. The ice show money was in it.

Forty-five dollars. That's what Patty had said.

Enough to buy a Tessie Dreamhouse.

No one was looking at Hilary or the cookie tin. Quickly, Hilary scooped up the tin and ran into her room with it. Her heart was pounding.

Hilary yanked on the middle drawer of her dresser. The drawer jerked forward. She cleared a spot in the back. She put the tin there and then buried it with clothing.

A wave of guilt washed over Hilary.

She tried to ignore it. She'd be rich someday. Then she'd pay them back. She'd pay them four hundred dollars. Each.

She pushed the drawer closed. Then she left the room and went to join the others.

6

A Thief in the House

HILARY GLANCED at the living room clock. It was almost eleven. She picked at her thumbnail as Mr. Baker spoke to the family. They were all there. Except for Dixie and Jack, who were asleep, and Kevin. He had returned from the hospital with his arm in a cast and wanted to go straight to bed.

Now they were talking about the missing money.

"This is very serious," said Mr. Baker.

"We have to be able to trust one another. Without trust, this family is in big trouble."

Mr. Baker looked sad. He sat on the arm of the old couch. His large hands rested on his knees.

"Maybe Patty forgot where she left the tin," said Collette.

Patty sat on the couch next to Mr. Baker. She wore her flannel nightgown. "I came into the hall. I put it down. And when I came back upstairs, it was gone."

"Does this mean we can't go to the ice show?" asked Terry. She sat on the floor next to Christine. Her large blue eyes seemed ready to overflow with tears.

Dad will pay for the tickets now, thought Hilary.

"I guess not," said Mr. Baker. "I don't think you kids can save enough money in one week. Of course, maybe someone will return the money."

"I'm going to get whoever did this!" cried Howie. "Whoever you are, give the money back."

"Simmer down, son," said Mr. Baker. "This is a first-time crime. If whoever took the money leaves it out in the open, we won't ask any questions."

"Should I keep collecting more money?" asked Patty.

"How do we know you didn't take it?" said Collette.

"Collette!" cried Christine. "That's mean."

"I wasn't being mean," said Collette. "It's just that Patty had the money last. She's the one who had the best chance to take it."

Patty's mouth opened and closed, but no sound came out. "I didn't," she muttered. "I don't steal."

"Wait till we get the creep who did this," said Howie.

"Wait a minute," Mrs. Baker said. "The person who took the money is still a member of this family. And we love you. No matter which one of you it is. You made a mistake. Now fix the mistake by returning the money. That's all."

A small lump formed in Hilary's throat. Part of her wanted to confess.

But she couldn't. She *had* to have that Dreamhouse.

"All right troops, to bed," said Mr. Baker. The kids got up and went to their rooms.

That night, Hilary found it hard to sleep. She couldn't get comfortable. Finally, she was about to drift off, when she heard a small sound.

Hilary sat up and listened. It was a sniffling sound. Patty was crying.

Hilary went over to Patty's bed. Patty was sobbing into the pillow. "What's the matter?" asked Hilary.

Patty lifted her head. In the moonlight Hilary could see her tearstained face. At her side, Patty held her rag doll, Zanzibar Marie. Hilary knew Patty must feel very bad. When she held Zanzibar Marie that tight, it meant she was upset.

"They all think I took it," said Patty. "I've only been here a month and a half. And I *did* have the money last. But I didn't take it. I really didn't."

"Collette shouldn't have said that," said Hilary. "A lot of times she just says dumb stuff without thinking."

Patty put Zanzibar Marie down on the bed. She began to cry again. "And just when things were going so good, too," she said through her tears.

Hilary sighed. "Things are good. Everybody likes you. You're a real Baker now, so don't worry about it."

"They think I'm a thief," Patty sobbed.

"Oh, cut it out," Hilary scolded. "I don't think you took the money."

"You don't?" asked Patty, looking up at Hilary.

"No."

"Who do you think did take it?" Patty asked her.

"I have no idea," Hilary snapped. "Now go to sleep. All this crying is keeping me awake."

Patty wiped her eyes with the sleeve of her nightgown. "Sorry," she sniffed.

Hilary climbed back into her bed. She pulled her blanket up over her shoulders and closed her eyes.

"Hilary?" Patty called to her gently.

"What? asked Hilary in a grouchy voice.

"I feel better. Thanks," said Patty.

"Go to sleep, will you," said Hilary.

7

The Dreamhouse

THE NEXT MORNING, the Baker kids walked down to the bus together. Everyone was very quiet.

On the bus, Hilary saw that Snoddy was absent. She turned to Patty. "Could you sit by yourself this morning? Pretty please," Hilary begged. "Snoddy isn't here and I have to talk to Alice."

"All right," Patty agreed. "Since Snoddy isn't here."

When Alice got on the bus, Hilary smiled at her.

Alice's eyes flickered angrily. She walked past Hilary and took the empty seat beside Patty. She began reading a book.

Patty looked over at Hilary. Their eyes met.

Hilary mouthed the words: *Switch seats.*

Patty rolled her eyes. But she got up. "Excuse me," she said to Alice as she squeezed past her.

"Thanks," Hilary whispered to Patty as they crossed in the aisle.

Hilary sat down beside Alice. The girl didn't look up.

"Don't be mad at me," Hilary pleaded. "I didn't mean for you to get into trouble."

"Oh, sure," said Alice. "Now I'm in trouble with my parents."

"I'll explain everything to your mother. I'll see her at the party Saturday," Hilary said.

"The party!" cried Alice, with a small

hoot of laughter. "You're not invited to the party anymore."

Not invited to the party! This couldn't be happening.

"But Alice," said Hilary. "I was going to get you a great gift."

"Like what?" asked Alice.

Hilary whispered into Alice's ear. "The Tessie Dreamhouse."

Alice's eyes opened wide. Then they narrowed. "You're lying," she said.

"I'm not lying," Hilary told her. "I was going to buy it today. I have the money right here in my pocket." Hilary lifted up her sweater and pulled out the corner of a bill.

"You know," Alice said, "I was only kidding about not inviting you to the party."

"I knew that," said Hilary.

"My mother is going to pick me up again today," said Alice. "We're going to Johnson's department store. They sell the Dreamhouse there. Do you want to come?"

"That would be great," replied Hilary. Finally, things were going right. Hilary hadn't figured out how to get to the store to buy the Dreamhouse. She wasn't allowed to go downtown by herself. Now the problem was solved.

The school day went slowly for Hilary. But at last it ended. Hilary called home to say that she was going to Alice's house after school. She asked to be picked up at five.

Mrs. Birmingham arrived in her beautiful car. She drove them to Johnson's.

Hilary watched while Alice tried on five different party dresses. Each dress was prettier than the next.

After Alice finally chose the nicest one, they went to the toy department. The Tessie Dreamhouse was so gigantic that the salesclerk had to take it off the shelf for them.

"This is a very generous gift," commented Mrs. Birmingham. "Does your mother always buy such expensive presents for parties?"

Hilary sensed that this was a trick question. Adults were always asking questions like this to trap kids. She had to think fast. "I added my own money to the money my mother gave me," she lied.

Mrs. Birmingham seemed to accept this. "Well, it's very nice of you," she said.

"It's okay," said Hilary. "Alice is one of my very best friends. I don't mind."

The cashier rang up the sale. Hilary suddenly realized she had another problem.

How was she going to get the Tessie Dreamhouse home?

"The kids at my house will wreck this," Hilary said to Mrs. Birmingham. "Can I leave it at your house?"

Mrs. Birmingham agreed.

Alice smiled brightly at Hilary. "You're such a good friend," she said.

When Hilary got home, she was the only one in a good mood. Everyone else seemed sad.

That night Olivia came to the bedroom to collect for the ice show. Hilary was doing homework. Patty was in the bathroom. "Why isn't Patty collecting the money?" Hilary asked.

"She said she didn't want to do it anymore," Olivia replied.

"Here," said Hilary. "I have some money for the ice show." Hilary took four dollars and twenty cents from the top of her dresser. It was the change from the Tessie Dreamhouse.

"Where did you get all that?" asked Olivia.

Hilary put the money in the tin. "It's my secret savings."

Olivia wrote down the amount Hilary had given. "If we don't save enough, we all get our money back," she said.

As Olivia left, Patty came in from the bathroom. Her wet hair was neatly wrapped in a towel turban.

"How come you aren't collecting anymore?" Hilary asked her.

"I'm scared that the money will get stolen again."

"It won't," said Hilary.

"How do you know?" Patty said, unwrapping her hair. "The thief might strike again."

Patty blew her hair dry. Then they turned out the lights. Hilary tried to think about the party tomorrow. She tried to imagine how proud she'd feel.

Alice would tell everyone: "Hilary Baker bought me this. She's my best friend."

Finally, she fell asleep.

"Help! Leave me alone! You can't have it!" someone screamed.

Hilary's eyes shot open.

At first, she didn't know what was

going on. She rubbed her eyes. Patty was asleep in the next bed. Then the scream turned into sobs. Hilary got out of bed. She left the room and followed the sound down the dark hall.

She went to the second floor. The door to Dixie's room was open, and a soft light shone out into the hallway.

Hilary went to the doorway. Mrs. Baker sat on the edge of the bed. She held Dixie on her lap. The night-light threw gentle shadows all over the room.

"I saw robbers," Dixie told her mother. "They took all my toys. And my books — even my Berry Bear coloring book."

Mrs. Baker stroked Dixie's blonde head. "She had a nightmare," Mrs. Baker said to Hilary.

Hilary picked a Berry Bear coloring book off the floor. "It's still here, Dixie," she said, handing Dixie the book.

Rubbing her eyes, Dixie took the book. "There are no robbers in the house, sweetheart," Mrs. Baker told her.

"Yes," Dixie insisted. "The bad person who took our money."

Mrs. Baker hugged Dixie tighter. "That person won't take your things," she said.

Dixie yawned. She leaned her head against her mother's chest. "Hilary, honey, you get back to bed," said Mrs. Baker. "Thanks for coming down."

"Okay," said Hilary. "Good night."

She climbed the stairs back up to her room. Poor Dixie. She didn't feel safe in her own room anymore.

Hilary opened her bedroom door. Moonlight shone through the window. In its light, she could see Patty sitting up in bed. "Where did you go?" asked Patty.

"Dixie had a nightmare. She woke me up," said Hilary.

Hilary sat on the end of Patty's bed. She couldn't take this anymore. She felt too guilty.

"Patty," she began. "I have to tell you something. It's something terrible."

"You took the money," Patty guessed.

"How did you know?" asked Hilary.

"Because it's the most terrible thing I could think of."

They sat in silence for a moment. "You're going to give it back, aren't you?" Patty said.

"I can't," Hilary told her sadly. "I would if I could."

"Why can't you?" cried Patty.

Hilary put her hand over Patty's mouth. "Shhhhhh! I don't want everyone to know." She told Patty about the Dreamhouse. "Alice already has it. What can I do?"

"I don't know," said Patty. "But we have to think of something."

8

The Party

"BE CAREFUL WITH THIS," Collette told Hilary. She held out her new yellow dress. Hilary had asked to borrow it for the party.

"I will," Hilary said, taking the dress from her.

Collette folded her arms. She studied Hilary. "You don't look very excited about this party," she said.

"I don't feel so good this morning," said Hilary. It was true. The thought of going to this party was making her sick.

"I don't feel so good, either," Collette said. "I had bad dreams all last night." She turned and left the room.

Hilary sighed.

"Here's the present," said Patty, coming into the room. She handed Hilary the doll dress their mother had bought. Patty had gift wrapped it.

"Alice will hate this present," said Hilary. She plopped down onto the floor. "This is the worst day of my life."

Patty pulled Hilary to her feet. "Come on. Remember what we planned. Tell Alice that you promised the Dreamhouse to a group of needy children."

"She won't believe that," Hilary whined.

"Who cares what she believes!" said Patty. "We have to get that present back."

The two girls got dressed. Patty had agreed to go to the party with Hilary. That way she wouldn't chicken out.

They met Mrs. Baker in the front hall.

"I didn't know you were invited," Mrs. Baker said to Patty.

"I invited her," said Hilary. "You know how close Patty and I are."

"All right," said Mrs. Baker doubtfully. "Get in the van."

Mrs. Baker dropped them off at Alice's house. Slowly, Patty and Hilary climbed the front steps to the porch.

They heard party sounds coming from inside. Patty raised her hand to knock on the door. Hilary grabbed it. "Let's get out of here," she said. "We can run away and hide out until Mom comes back."

"Forget it," said Patty, knocking on the door.

Alice came to the door. She looked especially pretty in her new party dress. She didn't seem happy to see Patty. "I asked Patty to come, okay?" said Hilary.

Alice looked at the present Patty held. "I guess so," she said. "Come on in."

They stepped into the wide front hall. In the living room girls from their class chattered happily. Rock music played. Bowls filled with potato chips and candy covered the table.

In the corner of the room was a pile of brightly wrapped gifts. Hilary spotted the Dreamhouse. Mrs. Birmingham had put a large red ribbon on it.

"Alice, I have to talk to you," said Hilary.

"What is it?" Alice asked.

Hilary stared at Patty. Her mind was blank. She couldn't find the words.

"We have a problem about the Dreamhouse," Patty spoke up.

"What kind of problem?" asked Alice, narrowing her eyes.

"Hilary needs the Dreamhouse back," Patty told her. "She brought you another present."

"You can't take a present back!" cried Alice.

Some of the girls stopped talking. They turned toward Alice, Hilary, and Patty.

"You see, Alice," said Patty. "We know a girl with a mystery disease. Her one wish is for a Tessie Dreamhouse. And — "

"Thanks for trying, Patty," said Hilary. "It's time I started telling the truth. Alice, I can't afford to give you the Dreamhouse. So I need to return it."

Alice's hands went to her hips. "I knew you lied about being rich," she said.

"Does it matter that much?" Patty asked.

Alice turned away. "I'm not giving the present back," she said. "You can't make me."

Now everyone was staring at them. "What's going on?" asked Mrs. Birmingham, coming into the hallway.

"My sister needs her present back," Patty told her. "We brought another."

Mrs. Birmingham seemed confused. But she went and got the Dreamhouse. "Here you go. Now come in and have some soda."

"No, thanks," said Hilary. "I think we should go. 'Bye, Alice. I'm sorry."

Alice didn't answer. She turned and went into her party. Hilary and Patty carried the Dreamhouse out the door. They didn't talk as they walked to Johnson's department store.

The saleslady took back the Dreamhouse. She handed Hilary forty dollars and eighty cents.

It was only one-thirty. They found a pay phone in the store. Patty called home. She asked their mother to pick them up at Alice's. "Can you come in about fifteen minutes?" she asked.

"Sure," said Mrs. Baker. "Are you girls all right?"

"Fine," Patty told her.

They walked back toward Alice's house. "Thanks," Hilary said to Patty. "I couldn't have done it alone. Poor Alice."

"Poor Alice!" Patty yelled. "All she wanted was the Dreamhouse. She doesn't care about being your friend. Don't you see that?"

Hilary hung her head. She knew Alice had used her. And it felt terrible.

"You don't have to buy friends, Hilary," said Patty. "Not real friends, anyway."

"I wanted so much for Alice to like me," said Hilary. "Now she'll never be my friend."

"You don't need a friend like Alice," said Patty.

"I suppose not," Hilary agreed sadly.

Patty gave Hilary a playful shove. "Come on," she said. "Let's meet Mom at the front of Alice's driveway."

Hilary began to run. "Okay," she said. "I'll race you." Side by side, the two girls ran back to Alice's.

9

A Happy Return

HILARY PUT THE MONEY in an envelope. When no one was looking, she laid it on top of the TV. Surely someone would notice it there.

But that had been a half hour ago. No one had gone near the TV. They were all busy finishing their Saturday chores.

"Is everyone blind?" Hilary whispered to Patty.

"Don't worry," said Patty. She walked near the TV. "Hey, look at this!" she shouted. "Does this belong to anyone?"

Christine came in from the hall. She took the envelope from Patty. "It's the money!" she cried.

The Baker kids came running from all over the house. "Are you sure?" asked Mrs. Baker, hurrying in from the kitchen.

Christine counted the money. "There's forty dollars and eighty cents here. There's four dollars and twenty cents still missing."

"Four dollars and twenty cents!" said Olivia. She looked sharply at Hilary.

Hilary froze. That was the exact amount she'd put in the collection tin. Now Olivia knew she was the thief. Would she tell the others?

Olivia turned and walked out of the room.

"What's going on?" asked Mr. Baker, walking into the room.

"The money came back," cried Jack.

Mr. Baker looked at his children. "I'm

proud of whichever one of you returned this money. I hope you'll never do this again and that you've learned your lesson," he said.

I sure have, thought Hilary.

But what was Olivia doing? Where had she gone?

At that moment, Olivia returned with her collection tin. "I collected nine dollars more," she said.

"That's a lot," said Kenny.

"Well, I had one big donation from Hilary," Olivia told them. She checked the piece of paper she had folded in her tin.

Hilary's heart pounded. Here it came. When Olivia said that she had given four dollars and twenty cents they would all know she had taken the money.

But Olivia didn't say anything else.

Hilary sighed with relief. *Thank you, Olivia,* she thought.

Howie pushed his glasses up on his nose. "Let's see how much we have." He looked to the ceiling as he added. "Forty dollars and eighty cents, plus nine is forty-nine eighty. Plus Mom's seventy is one hundred and nineteen dollars and eighty cents. We need one hundred and eighty. Which means we have to come up with . . . sixty dollars and twenty cents."

"We'll never make it," said Kevin, hitting his cast against the couch.

"Hold on," cried Chris, running from the room. She soon returned with an envelope. "I got this today from China!" she told them. "Granny Baker sent it to me for my birthday. Thirty-five dollars." She put the check into the tin.

"That's my mom," laughed Mr. Baker. "On top of things even while she's traveling."

"That leaves twenty-five dollars and twenty cents," Howie told them.

Mr. Baker dug into his pocket. He threw a twenty and a five into the tin. "Here. I think this will help a little."

"Twenty cents left," said Howie.

"I found it!" cried Dixie. She had been digging in the sofa cushions. She now had two nickels and a dime.

Proudly, she dropped them into the tin.

"We made it!" yelled Collette, jumping into the air.

"We're going to the ice show!" cried Terry, bouncing up and down.

Hilary watched as her family cheered and jumped and kissed one another. Patty and Olivia spun in a circle.

She felt lucky to have sisters like them! What a wonderful family she had!

Hilary knew she would always long for pretty things. She'd always want more than she had.

But right now, Hilary felt very very rich.